Those Amazing Ants

by Patricia Brennan Demuth
illustrated by S. D. Schindler

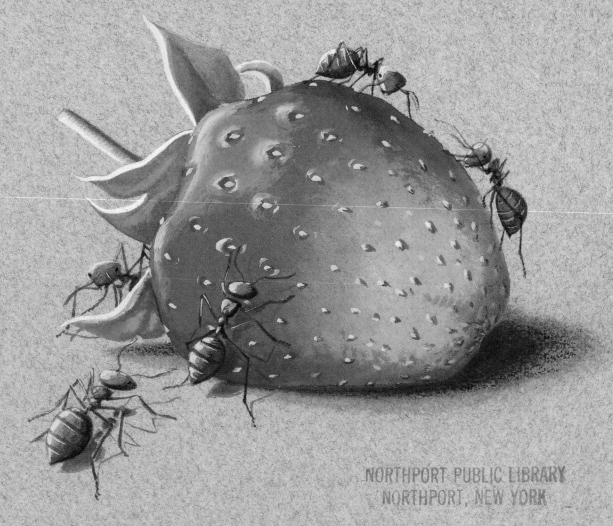

Macmillan Publishing Company   New York
Maxwell Macmillan Canada   Toronto
Maxwell Macmillan International   New York   Oxford   Singapore   Sydney

Library of Congress Cataloging-in-Publication Data
Demuth, Patricia Brennan. Those Amazing Ants / by Patricia Brennan Demuth ; illustrated
by S. D. Schindler. — 1st ed.   p.   cm.   Summary: Describes those fascinating insects, the ants,
in simple words and pictures.   ISBN 0-02-728467-0   1. Ants—Juvenile literature.   [1. Ants.]
I. Schindler, S. D., ill.   II. Title.   QL568.F7D46   1994   595.79′6—dc20   93-1769
1   3   5   7   9   10   8   6   4   2

For the terrific Reinhard trio:
Bill, Andy, and Katy
—P.B.D.

All the ants you see walking around are
females—girl ants.
So whenever you see an ant, you can
call it *she*!

Did you ever stand near an anthill and watch
ants disappear down the little hole?
What do they do when they get under the ground?
What's it like down there?

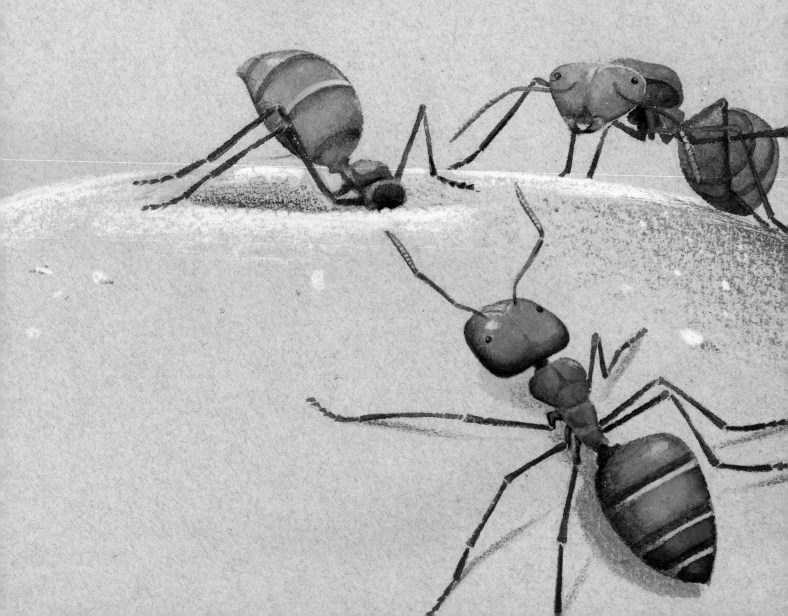

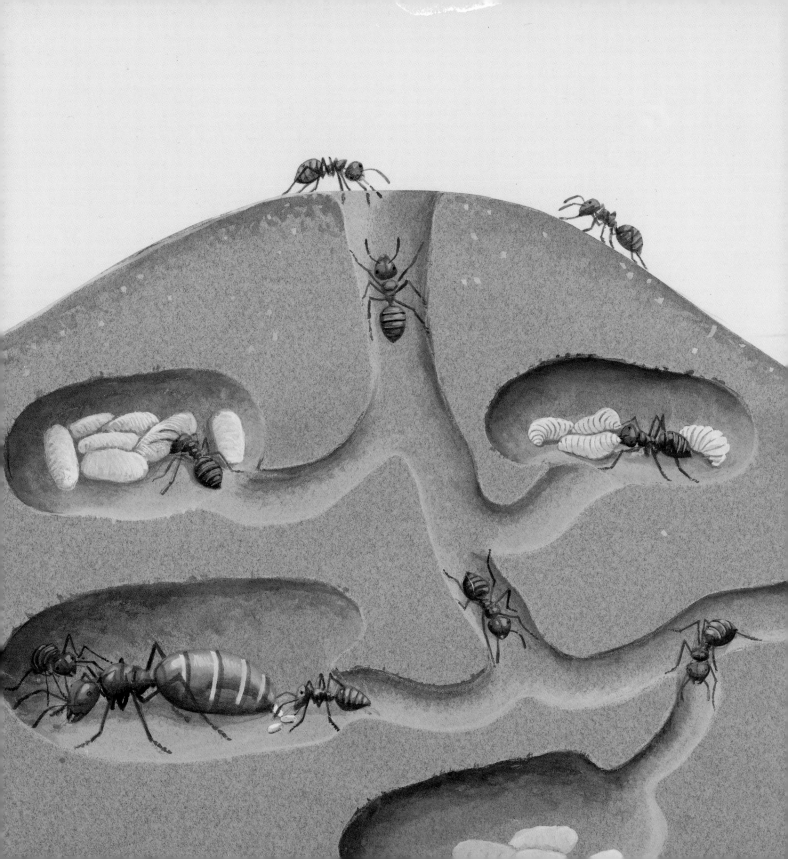

The ants' home is down there under the ground.
The home has little rooms dug out of the dirt.
All the rooms are connected by tunnels.
Some ant homes are huge.
They have hundreds of rooms on different
levels—like an apartment building.

The ants make all the rooms and tunnels
by digging with their legs.
They throw out the dirt that is left over.
That dirt becomes the anthill.

Every room has a special use.
One is a sickroom.
Ants that are hurt stay there.
Another room is a pantry
for storing food.

The nursery is reserved for baby ants.

And still another room is reserved for the queen.

Every ant home has its own queen.
She is bigger than the other ants.
She has only one job: to lay all the eggs.
The other ants treat their queen like royalty.
They wait on her.
They feed her.
They rub her back.
They even bathe her.

Babies get just as much care as the queen does.
Certain ants in the home are baby-sitters.
Their job is to watch over the baby ants at all times.

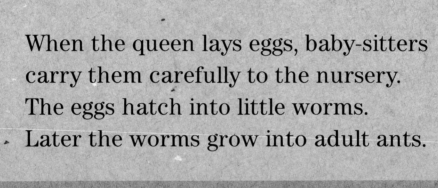

When the queen lays eggs, baby-sitters
carry them carefully to the nursery.
The eggs hatch into little worms.
Later the worms grow into adult ants.

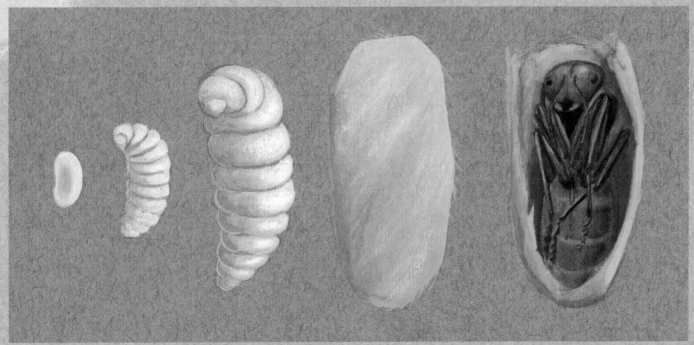

Baby-sitters lick the babies to keep them clean.
Ants have tiny tongues for this purpose.
They feed the babies with food from their own
stomachs.
On a nice day, baby-sitters may carry the little
ones outside to get some sunlight.

Other ants keep busy, too.
Finding food is one big job.
An ant leaves the nest to search around.
The little feelers on top of her head wiggle
in the air.
Why?
Because her "nose" is inside the feelers!
The ant is smelling for food when
she waves her feelers around.

When an ant finds food, she gets very excited.
She knows her family will want to come and get
some of the food, too.
So on the way home, she lays down a path of tiny drops
by touching the tip of her body to the ground.

Other ants can smell these drops and follow her
trail—all the way back to the food.
If there's lots of food, hundreds of ants
will pour out of the anthill and go get it.
They march in two long lines: one leading from
the anthill to the food, and one back again.

Ants do take time out to nap.
They fold up their six legs and their feelers
and sleep snugly.
When an ant wakes up, she yawns and
stretches—just as you do.

Then the ant grooms herself.
An ant likes to keep her body clean,
especially her feelers.
She cleans them with little combs on her
front legs.
She licks other parts of her body, just
like a cat does.
If she cannot reach a spot, an ant will rub
against something to get the dirt off.

Ants often clean and comb each other, too. They seem to relax this way, just as you might enjoy a back rub.

Ants keep their homes clean and tidy.
They won't bear any mess.
Most ants have a dumping ground outside their homes.
They bury all their trash in the dump.

These ants are soldiers.
They make war against other ants.
They capture enemies and make them slaves.

These ants keep other insects—just like farmers keep cows.
The ants "milk" the insects by rubbing their backs.
A sweet liquid comes out. It is called honeydew.

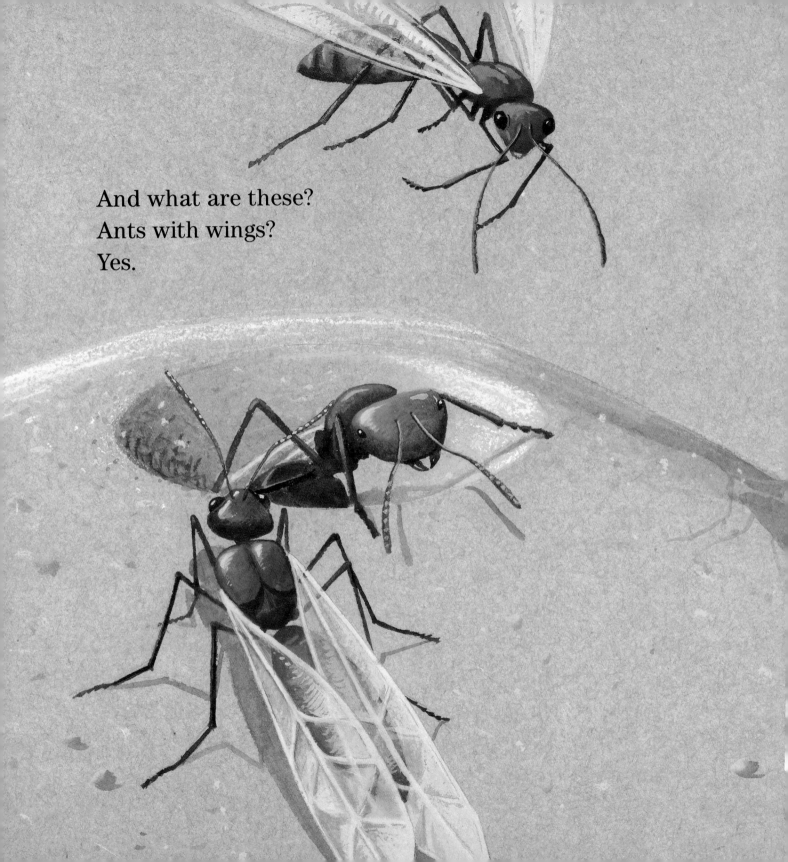

And what are these?
Ants with wings?
Yes.

These are *male* ants.
Their only job in life is to mate with the queen.
That's why they have wings.
These male ants need to fly to catch the queen
on her mating flight.
Afterward the male ants die.
Their job is done.
But the job of the queen has just begun.
After the mating flight, the queen rips off her wings.
She lays her first batch of eggs.
From then on, that's all she will do—just lay eggs.
Some ant queens live for fifteen years and lay
millions of eggs.

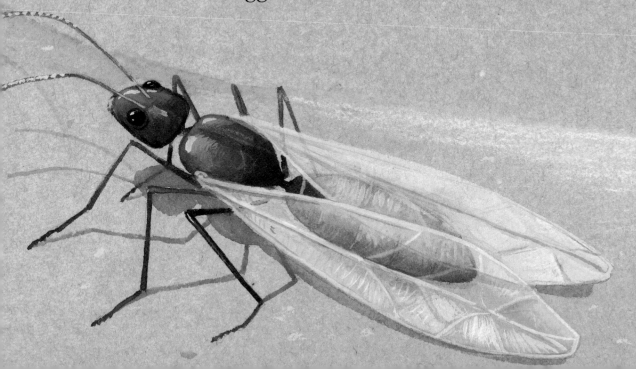

Ants are bitty creatures.
Yet they are amazing, don't you agree?

DATE			